Pro

ALSO BY K. J. PARKER

The Devil You Know
The Last Witness
The Company
The Folding Knife
The Hammer
Sharps
Purple and Black
Blue and Gold
Savages
The Two of Swords
Academic Exercises (collection)

THE FENCER TRILOGY
Colours in the Steel
The Belly of the Bow
The Proof House

THE SCAVENGER TRILOGY
Shadow
Pattern
Memory

THE ENGINEER TRILOGY

Devices and Desires
Evil for Evil
The Escapement

AS TOM HOLT (SELECTED TITLES)

Expecting Someone Taller
Who's Afraid of Beowulf?
Flying Dutch
Faust Among Equals
Snow White and the Seven Samurai
Valhalla
The Portable Door
You Don't Have to Be Evil to Work Here, But It Helps
The Better Mousetrap
Blonde Bombshell
The Outsorcerer's Apprentice
The Good, the Bad, and the Smug

PROSPER'S
DEMON

K . J . P A R K E R

A TOM DOHERTY ASSOCIATES BOOK

NEW YORK

PROSPER'S DEMON

Copyright © 2019 by Tom Holt

Cover art by Sam Weber
Cover design by Christine Foltzer

Edited by Jonathan Strahan

A Tor.com Book
Published by Tom Doherty Associates
120 Broadway
New York, NY 10271

www.tor.com

Tor® is a registered trademark of
Macmillan Publishing Group, LLC.

ISBN 978-1-250-26050-5 (ebook)
ISBN 978-1-250-26051-2 (trade paperback)

First Edition: January 2020

After many unhappy experiments in the direction of an ideal Republic, it was found that what may be described as Despotism tempered by Dynamite provides the most satisfactory description of ruler. . . .

—**W. S. Gilbert**

Prosper's Demon

I WOKE TO FIND her lying next to me, quite dead, with her throat torn out. The pillow was shiny and sodden with blood, like low-lying pasture after a week of heavy rain. The taste in my mouth was familiar, revolting, and unmistakable. I spat into my cupped hand: bright red. Oh, for crying out loud, I thought. Here we go again.

I crawled out of bed and tried to get my sleepy brain working. Some people are galvanized into decisive action by a crisis. I get all fogged up, like a cart stuck in soft ground; the wheels turn and turn, but no traction.

Blood *spreads*; you can't seem to confine it, no matter how you try. So I took a leaf out of the First Emperor's book and built a huge circumvallatory wall, out of fabric—sheets, curtains, the hangings off the walls, all my shirts except the one I was wearing (which was ruined, too, of course)—practically every fiber in the house. By gradually closing this cloth embankment in around the bed, I managed to keep the blood from getting on the walls and the doors, where it'd be sure to leave an indelible mark. Trust me, I know all about blood; every time a sheet or a curtain got soaked through, I wrapped it in something else and shifted it to the upper layer of the heap. The body itself went on the very top, like a beacon on a mountain peak. Luckily the floor was marble, about the only substance on earth blood doesn't soak into permanently. I wrapped the body up in a beautiful and rather expensive Aelian rug I'd bought only a week earlier, then tied it tight with string.

To get the whole horrible mess out of the door, I used a modification of the travois principle: a heavy-duty coir mat, which I happened to have by me for some reason or other, with two holes stabbed in two corners to pass a rope through. It slid along quite nicely across the smooth marble floor and left only a few rusty brown streaks, which were no bother at all to wipe up afterwards. Out the side door, then just a matter of lifting the ghastly bale of ruined textiles and the rolled-up rug into my eight-hundred-gulden fancy chaise (served me right for indulging myself; I make a lot of money, and I'm always broke), harnessing up the horse, and off we went. There's a worked-out quarry two miles or so from where I was living at the time. Sheer sides, deep, and the bottom is grown over with briars and withies and rubbish. I got the horse out of the shafts, put my shoulder to the back wheel, and sent my lovely expensive chaise tumbling over the edge. It disappeared into the tangle like a stone sinking in a pond. Job done.

On the ride home, I looked down at my hands, and I thought: It's a bit much. If you can't trust your own hands, what can you trust? Except I can't, not after the last time, or the time before that. One of Them had crept inside me while I was asleep and taken control of my hands away from me, used them to murder a young woman, practically a stranger, whose only crime was a little commercialized affection. In this jurisdiction, the worst you get for that is a two-thaler fine and a morning in the stocks (and that's excessive, if you ask me). Instead, a savage and violent death, at my hands. *My* hands, you bastard. I'll have you for that.

My fault, for thinking I could get away with even a cash-down travesty of ordinary human feeling; my fault for involving a civilian. I thought about that and looked at my short, stubby fingers, used against me like a club snatched from a watchman's belt by a violent drunk. Not my fault, I decided. Never mine. Always His.

$\sim$

I have an idea you aren't going to like me very much.

That may prove to be the only thing we'll have in common, so let's make the most of it. I do terrible things. I do them to my enemies, to my own side, to myself. In the process, I save a large number of strangers (on average, between five and ten a week) from the worst thing that can happen to a human being. I'd like to say I do it because I'm one of the good guys, but if I did that, you'd see right through me. And then you'd quote scripture at me: Render to no one evil for evil.

Really? Even if they're the enemy? Even if They're not human?

You decide. Not sure I can be bothered with it anymore.

~

I have one thing in common with the Emperor: I was born into a certain line of work, without the faintest possibility of choice. A blacksmith's son might just possibly decide to run away and enlist or join a troupe of traveling actors or pick cotton or beg on street corners. Not me. Like the heir apparent, I can't just melt away into the crowd. I'd be recognized, found out, forced back to my honors and obligations. And as for not doing the work I was born to do; inconceivable. Might as well say, it's entirely up to me whether I breathe or not.

It's a commonplace in the trade that ours is a lonely existence; perfectly true. The first thing you do, on discovering that you have the gift (the word *gift* here used in its technical sense, meaning the ability, as opposed to something anyone in his right mind might conceivably want to be given), is to run away from home, severing all ties with your previous life. This is, it goes without saying, absolutely essential. When I left home, I stole my father's gold signet ring, all my mother's jewelry, and my sister's silk shawl, which she loved more than anything else in the world. I had to. As a family we were comfortable but hardly well-off, and I needed small, portable items that could be turned into money quickly and without fuss. With the proceeds I booked a passage on a lumber barge. Didn't bother asking where it was going. The point being: They can go anywhere on land, but They can't cross salt water. Small mercies.

Actually, now I think about it, I have something else in common with His Serenity. I have absolute authority. Lucky, lucky me.

~

I knew He couldn't have gone far. They can't; They get hungry as soon as They leave a human host, and hunger makes Them weak. He wouldn't be hard to find, and after pulling off a prank like that, He'd be relatively quiet and peaceful for a day or so. So I went home, had a good wash, brushed my teeth thoroughly (first with soot, then with myrrh and peppermint); packed up my remaining possessions and loaded them into the donkey cart—it was only then that it occurred to me that I could have sacrificed the donkey cart instead of the chaise and it'd have done just as well. His fault, of course. All His fault.

I'm used to moving on at short notice. Plenty of practice, over the years, and I'm uniquely adapted to a life without roots and connections, although wherever I go, I know exactly whom I'm going to meet, sooner or later. Objectively speaking, needless to say, it's a wonderful thing that there are so few of Them—otherwise, the human race would be over and done with, finished. But for me, it means I have to deal with the same old faces (so to speak) over and over and over again, until They're sick of me and I'm sick of Them. And believe me, I'm sick to death of Them, especially when They pull stunts like that.

My luck was in. The first small town I came to, it was market day. I sold the donkey cart, the donkey, and all my worldly goods at not too unbearable a loss, leaving me with sixteen gulden forty-seven, plus the value of one bloodstained shirt, one coarse brown ecclesiastical gown, and a pair of army boots. When you think what I charge for even a run-of-the-mill, in-and-out-in-five-minutes, everyday kind of job, it'd reduce some men to floods of tears, but fortunately I'm not really bothered. Money, things have never really mattered to me very much. Incredibly difficult come, easy go—so what? It's a bit like being the biggest landowner on an island dominated by an active volcano. You know it's always just a matter of time.

When I arrive in a new place, I try really hard not to notice Them, but it's impossible. I can't help it, like a dog in a field of sheep. Actually, make that a dog in an alleyful of cats, and it's not a bad analogy. It's the same unthinking, instinctive, bred-in-the-bone antipathy, and They don't like me much either. I catch sight of Them in the farthest corner of my peripheral vision, and I can't help it; I point, people tell me, like a hunting dog.

Note peripheral vision. They know when I'm coming, and They freeze, dead still, not a flicker. Sure, I know They're in the neighborhood, I can smell Them. I can track Them down by smell alone, if I have to, though it very rarely comes to that, obviously. But when I walk down the street, the most I ever see is that tiny flicker of movement right on the extreme edge. And that's all I need.

But the hell with it. It's all about being professional, and not being on duty. Poets don't write hexameters on their day off, whores don't make love, soldiers don't kill people; I can't help noticing, but I'm under no obligation to do anything about it, particularly when I'm not getting paid. Not unless—

I heard a woman scream. Reluctantly, I turned my

head. A man was lying on the ground, his back arched, his heels dragging furrows in the mud. His face was just starting to turn blue, and the crotch of his trousers was sodden wet. A dozen or so people were forming a loose ring around him, backing away. He made that unmistakable noise. It's not an actual shout or yell; it's purely mechanical, the muscles in spasm forcing air out of the lungs through a tightly constricted throat. Another unique sound: the sharp dry-stick crack of a bone, broken by the monstrous contraction of its own muscles and sinews.

Hence, I guess, the dog-and-cat reaction. Possibly it's just that I find it offensive when one of Them dares do Its stuff when I'm there, as though I'm nobody, don't count for anything, chopped liver. I prefer to put it down to compassion, and an undying hostility toward the Common Enemy of Man. But I would say that, wouldn't I?

Five long strides brought me up close enough. I looked in through the sides of the poor devil's head and caught Its eye. It stared back at me; always the same expression, like a bad boy in your apple tree with half of one of your apples in his mouth.

You again, It said.

Me, I replied.

That's the thing about our line of work. Some monk with far too little to do once calculated it exactly, using the very finest scriptural materials; there are 72,936 of

Them. Sounds a lot, except that's *all*. That's to cover, or service, or garrison—choose your inadequate and inappropriate verb—the entire human race, all fifteen *million* of us. And, of course, They have Their territories, as all predators do; like my fellow practitioners; like me. And, of course, They can't be killed or die—They just get moved on, like the poor—so, of course, I keep meeting Them, over and over and over again. And moving Them on. I have, after all, the authority.

~

It looked so sad and wistful. *Give me a break,* It said.

Out, I said.

I just got here.

Tough.

Five minutes, all right? Just give me five minutes and then I'll be on my way.

Out, I said.

I have the authority. Out, I say, and out They have to go. They go because They know that if They don't, I can haul Them out, I can reach in, inside, grab hold of Them by—God only knows what, let's just say They aren't put together quite the same as you and me—and drag Them out of there. When I do that, it hurts, rather a lot to judge by Their reaction, though for all I know They may have really low pain thresholds, or They may just make a lot of fuss about the littlest thing, like pigs.

But—you have to be careful. I can pull Them out; a bit like when you've got toothache so bad, you go to the blacksmith. And if he's a gentle, sensible man, he'll get a firm grip on it with his tongs and just turn his wrist, this way then that, then one quick, strong, controlled flick and it's all done and no bother. Or he could break your jaw, and still leave splinters of crushed tooth in there.

Makes you shudder just to think of it. Well, that's mouths. These things live in minds. So, as I said, you have to be careful.

Give me five minutes, It said.

At which point, you have to make a decision. You consider the amount of damage It's already done—in this case, a broken leg, because I'd heard it break, and almost certainly a rib or two, high chance of internal bleeding, the little bastards never can resist *playing*—and then you weigh the harm It'll do if you leave It in there a moment longer against the havoc It could cause if you have to yank It out. Factor against all that the pain and trauma It'll feel being extracted, of which It's so very, very scared; and then you ask yourself, is It really so tired and hungry that It'll risk being manhandled, or is It simply trying it on, the way They all do, 999 times in 1,000?

Which is why, in actual appalling fact, it's a good thing

that we have our territories and They have Theirs and we all get to know each other so terribly, terribly well—

No, I said. *Count of three. One—*

Not going.

Two.

The man—I think he was some sort of merchant, by his clothes and the fact I didn't know him—sprang to his feet. No, he was lifted to his feet, for the split second in question he was actually standing on his broken leg, it folded and he collapsed, and by the time he hit the ground it was all over, nobody in there who shouldn't be, no longer any business or interest of mine. I looked away and walked on.

And there's the thing. Anybody who happened to be watching me and not the motionless twisted wreck of a human being on the ground would have seen a man in a shabby priest's robe stop, gawp, and then pass on by—callous, unfeeling bastard, he'd say to himself; and who am I to contradict? I'd done my professional duty, and there my involvement ended. Sometimes I wonder if it's more that I hate Them than that I love my fellow humans. But nobody pays me to think that, so I don't do it often.

~

Scripture, about which I'm vaguely skeptical, tells us that when the Invincible Sun rose for the very first time, He drew up out of the marshes and swamps that covered the face of the Earth all the noxious, foul damps and vapors in which our universal Mother had been quietly marinating since the beginning of time; these vapors were promptly carried away on the breeze, and according to the highly respected authority I quoted just now, there are 72,936 of Them.

People ask me, I really wish they wouldn't, but they do: What do They look like? To which I give various replies, all untrue. Fact is, I don't know. When I ask the same annoying question of my professional peers, on the rare occasion that I meet one and we're on speaking terms, I get an answer, and I try and give an honest answer in return. To one practitioner They look like horrible insects; to another, ghastly, unnatural fish or rats, or disgusting birds, or shrunken, desiccated children. To me They look like shellfish. And all that proves is, beauty isn't the only mote in the beholder's eye.

More interesting is when you ask one of Them what we look like. But I digress.

Seventy-two thousand nine hundred thirty-six, of which 109 operate in my jurisdiction, which extends from the Charyabda Mountains to the Friendly Sea, mercifully excluding the cities of Bomyra, Euxis, and Bine

Seauton. Within that area, which comprises three tempo-
ral nation-states, at least two of which are at war with at
least two of the others at any given time, I'm licensed by
His Holiness to expel demons for money. To prove my
bona fides, I have a certificate with illuminated capitals
and a lead seal, which at least one in a thousand people
can read, and a gold ring with a white stone given to me
by the Metropolitan Cardinal. Correction, I have a piss-
poor imitation of same, a pebble set in brass, which I had
made for me when I lost the original. Thus my creden-
tials, and it's a funny thing. People never seem to ask to
see them before I operate; only afterwards, when they're
called upon to pay the bill.

Mostly, though, I don't bother, just as the dog doesn't
look round for someone to recompense him for chasing
the cat. Why should they believe it was me; and even if
they did, what can I do to them if they don't pay? Put
the bloody thing back where I found It? Actually, I have
made the empty threat before now, and it works like a
charm, but you can't always rely on people being de-
plorably ignorant.

So, having saved the merchant's soul and sanity and
probably his life, too, I passed by on the other side, with
nothing to show for it but the splitting headache They always give me afterwards. I went up the street to Haymar-
ket, and looked in at the Harmony & Grace.

"Oh," they said. "You again."

Inhospitable but fair enough: last time there had been an unfortunate incident, and the time before that, though not of my making. But they respect the gown and they know what the stupid brass ring stands for, and there's always the lurking fear at the back of their minds: better not to piss off this loathsome and troublesome man, just in case we need him one day. Which is why nobody is ever pleased to see me, and why I never have to buy my own drinks.

I told them I'd be staying for a while. How long, they asked sadly, is a while? I smiled and said I didn't know. Would that be a problem? No, they told me, no problem at all.

You have to learn to think like Them, they told me when I was just starting out in the business; only, don't get too good at it. They say that to all the students, and none of us really understand what it means at the time.

In and out of each other's heads, like neighbors in a small, friendly village, which is exactly what we aren't. Or, to put it another way, it doesn't do to get too familiar.

But it didn't take me long to figure out what He—

Excuse me, I have a lot of trouble with pronouns. The proper singular form for one of Them is, of course, It. We neither know nor care whether They are divided into genders as we are, nor, as far as I can tell, do They. But rules were made to be broken, at least as far as I'm concerned, and this one particular, unique, individual specimen was definitely, in my mind, a He. I don't know why; I suspect it has more to do with me than—well, Him. For some reason I need Him to be male in order to deal with Him. That's one of the many dangers I was warned about. Precisely because everybody sees Them differently, the risk is always of creating Them in your own image.

So, indulge me: Him. It didn't take me long to figure out what He was up to, or why He'd gone to all the trouble of attacking me. All I needed, therefore, was a copy of the *Court Circular* and a fast horse.

~

I told you that you wouldn't like me.

I understand. It shows proper feeling. If you said to me: There's this man who is so callous and brutal that he doesn't give a damn about his fellow human beings, wouldn't shed a tear over the death of an innocent; would you care to meet this person, shake hands with him, maybe invite him into your home and have dinner with him? You're kidding, right.

That hypothetical piece of shit is, of course, me. All my life—

~

Many of the great civilized nations have a foundation myth in which their national hero was abandoned on a hillside at birth and brought up by wolves, or bears or hyenas or whatever your local gregarious predator happens to be. To all intents and purposes I was brought up by *Them*. What the hell do you expect?

I feel guilty because I don't feel guilty. Sure, I could defend myself, if I wanted to. I could describe to you what it's like having one of Them inside your head. It hurts, like nothing else, all the time. It makes you do things, the sort of things you'll never forgive yourself for, even though you know it's not you doing them. You'd kill yourself to be rid of the pain and the shame and the dread of what you're going to do next, only *It won't let you*. It's torture and rape and all the worst things that can possibly happen, and it's not just suffering it but doing it to others, friends, lovers, children. It lays eggs of sheer horror deep inside you, and you can feel them hatching, growing, their burgeoning new life trapping your nerves against the bone.

I can tell you about that, and case histories of lives ruined, and lives saved when I intervene. But I'm not going to defend myself. I'm too far down the road for that. The victims aren't what motivates me, not anymore. Or not the only thing.

All I can do, am prepared to do, is ask you to consider two things: my motives and the effect of my actions. The effect of my actions is to save my brothers and sisters from the worst possible thing that can happen to anyone, and only I, and a handful of others like me, can do this. My motivations are my own business, my privilege and my intolerable burden.

~

The wedding of Grand Duke Sigiswald of Essen to the Princess Hildigunn, daughter of the Elector Frohvat of Risenem, was rather a low-key affair. There were ten thousand guests at the wedding breakfast, and all the fountains in Essen ran with sweet white wine, but that was about it. No triumphal procession, gladiatorial displays, mock sea battles, or mass sacrifice of prisoners of war on the Temple steps; no nationwide amnesty or emancipation of slaves; and only a modest donative, five gold kreutzer a man, to the soldiers in the army. Times, whispered the underlying message, are hard, money is tight, and your Duke and his lovely bride are setting an example.

The message was received loud and clear and went down well with the taxpayers, so that was all right. But the Princess insisted on one small indulgence. Unless she could be accompanied into the wilderness (her words, not mine) by her faithful tutor and confidant, Prosper of Schanz, she wasn't going, and her father and six years of eggshell-brittle diplomacy could go to hell.

No, it wasn't like that at all. Prosper was sixty if he was a day, and it took four strong men to prize him out of his chair and load him onto a specially reinforced chaise every time Her Highness felt like a spot of intellectual conversation. His salary at the time was sixty thousand kreutzer a year, and he insisted on a 50 percent raise to compensate him for leaving Risenem and going to live among the woad-painted savages (he'd said something similar when the Elector headhunted him from Falhoel), so he was rather more than a trivial whim. Ninety thousand would pay the Sixth Legion for a month, or fit out twelve warships. You'd have to have a heart of stone, though, if you didn't reckon Prosper of Schanz to be a bargain at three times the price. The finest painter and sculptor of his age, even though he very rarely finished anything; the most learned scholar, though everything he'd ever published fit neatly into one small, handy pocket edition; the most exquisite and refined musician; the most outstanding natural philosopher and engineer. By all accounts, Hildigunn had a tin ear, didn't like any painting that wasn't blue, and had to sign her name through a stencil, but she knew a class act when she saw one, and always had to have the best. So Prosper came to Essen, with all his books, machines, tin boxes full to bursting with notebooks and diaries, mechanical and philosophical paraphernalia, clogging up the mountain roads for a week. They say he spent his first month in residence watching a sheep's head decaying on a mounting block in the stable yard. He wanted to see for himself exactly how the process of deliquescence and entropy worked, in real time, second by second. So he had a comfortable chair brought down from the royal apartments on the sixth floor, and a footstool, a handy writing table, and a good supply of nice things to drink and snack on, and sat there, night and day (with a brazier to keep him warm and a huge silk umbrella to keep him dry), just watching. Whether the result was any special insight into the natures of change and mortality, I couldn't say, but you have to admit, the man's a class act, by any standards.

When the news broke that Sigiswald and Hildigunn had fulfilled their royal function and a tiny Elector was on the way, Prosper declared that this would be the ideal opportunity for him to put into practice a project that had been growing like a stalactite in the back of his godlike mind for absolutely ages: nothing less than the handcrafting of the ultimate superior human being—an enterprise, he modestly said, worthy of himself, at last.

Since he was the greatest living authority on obstetric medicine, Prosper announced that he would deliver the child himself. As soon as it was born, he would personally supervise every aspect of its upbringing, nurture, and education. He would mold the child in his own image, teach it everything he knew, with a view to giving the world its first true top-notch very-best-quality philosopher-king, who would in turn solve every problem, make the world into an earthly paradise, and serve as a fitting monument to the greatest man who ever lived.

Now, conceding that Prosper was at least 40 percent full of the stuff that makes roses grow, that still left quite a lot of sheer unparalleled genius. The royal parents, no doubt reflecting on their own childhoods and education and figuring that anything had to be better than that, announced that they were delighted to give the great man carte blanche.

They nailed up a new copy of the *Court Circular* on the front door of the Temple in Jasca on the first day of the month. The lead story was Hildigunn's due date. It gave me precisely six days to cover the two hundred miles of rutted roads and broken-down bridges to Essen, a miracle that I somehow managed to accomplish.

I was in a foul mood when I reached the palace gate. I bounced up to the sentry and told him I needed to see the duty officer. He looked at me, weighing my derelict boots against the priest's gown, and decided I was too difficult for him. That got me inside the lodge, where I hung around for most of the morning until the duty officer was available. Being an officer, he could read, so I showed him my certificate. It worried him. It's supposed to.

"How can I help you, Father?" he said.

"I need to see the palace chaplain," I told him. "Now."

I could see the poor man's brain grinding to a halt, as though I'd stuck an iron bar through the spokes. The chaplain, needless to say, wasn't part of his chain of command and he had no idea how to get in touch with him. Lucky for him, he had me to do his thinking for him. "You'll need to get a pass from the Prefect," I told him, "to take me inside so I can explain to the deputy chamberlain why I need to see the chaplain. He'll take it from there."

Joy unbounded for the duty officer, who whisked me up seven flights of winding narrow stone stairs to the Prefecture, where I spent far too long hanging about while my pass was written up. Then a sad-looking clerk led me down the stairs I'd just come up and up an even longer staircase to the chamberlain's office, where I showed my certificate to somebody's poor relation's younger son, who went white as a sheet and told me to follow him. Nine flights of winding narrow stone stairs up to the Chaplaincy, where the junior deputy chaplain asked me what I wanted.

"I want to see the chaplain."

"That's not possible right now."

"Yes," I told him. "Actually, it is."

So we went to see the chaplain, who scowled at my certificate as if it were a turd floating in his soup, and shut the door so nobody could hear us. "What?" he said.

"I need to see the Duchess," I told him.

"Nobody sees the Duchess."

Bless him, he was having a bad day, I could tell. He had twelve large-scale services to plan out, for at least three of which there was no clearly established precedent, which meant he was going to have to wing it, liturgically speaking, and hope nobody present would be sufficiently erudite to find him out. On top of that, me: a fully authorized representative of a branch of the Ministry that is always bad news at any time; at a time like this—

I'd have liked to help him out, but I couldn't afford to indulge myself. I sat there and stared at him, a bit like the Sun, which you're not supposed to look directly at.

"Why?" he said.

"Three guesses."

"You're not making any sense," he said. "Are you trying

to tell me that a member of the royal household is—?"

"Not yet."

"But that's absurd," he said. "It's impossible to predict when and where—"

"No," I told him, "it isn't."

People really don't like looking at me if they can possibly avoid it. There's something about me that makes me objectionable to have in their field of vision. The company I keep, presumably.

"I can't just admit you to the royal birth chamber," he said. "Not without very good reason and documentary evidence to corroborate—"

He tailed off. I was the worst thing that had ever happened to him in his entire life, and he'd done nothing whatever to deserve me. "All right," he said, "if you insist. But I'll be making a written memorandum that I'm doing this under protest."

Which was probably the most aggressive thing he'd ever said, and he watched it bounce off me like gravel off a breastplate. "When you're quite ready," I said.

"Follow me."

~

How far back can you remember? When you were a toddler? Before you could walk? Before you could speak, just possibly? I can trump that. I can remember before I was born. Being unborn, and not alone.

It was in there with me, you see; the first one I ever met. They're not stupid. They know where They're safe. If They can get inside a child before it's born, They know They've got security of tenure for at least ten years, maybe as many as twelve, because of the unspeakable level of collateral damage that would be involved in digging Them out. Works both ways, mind; leaving an infant hurts Them just as much as it hurts the host, so if They choose to enter an unborn child, They're stuck there until the child matures, and the pickings are slim. It's *boring,* living in something so small and crude and stupid, so They take that option only when They're hurt and need somewhere to hole up and recover, or when They've had a really rough ride at the hands of me and my lot. In my case, It had just been evicted, with rather more force than absolutely necessary, from Its previous home. It was smashed up and raw, a real mess, and It had just enough strength to crawl inside my mother before It passed out and collapsed; and then It encountered me.

I remember It very clearly. It was a voice I could understand, outside me but very close. *Let me in,* It said. *Please,* It said.

I can remember what it was like, thinking without words, knowing nothing—nothing at all. But It wanted to come inside me, and I didn't want It to. I pushed It away. It tried to push back, but It couldn't. *Go away,* I told It.

Oh, for crying out loud, It said. *You're one of them.*

I didn't understand, of course, but I didn't like it, not one little bit. I pushed It away. I could feel myself hurting It. It was the first thing I ever came across that was weaker than me, that I could prevail over, that I could hurt. It wasn't bothering me anymore, but I could bother It, if I wanted to. I wanted to. Good game. I pushed harder.

Stop that, It said. *You're hurting me.*

Go away, I told It, but I didn't mean it. I wanted It to stay and be played with. Rough games, the sort small children enjoy.

I'm stuck, It said, *I can't get out. Stop pushing.*

Memories are tricky; there's what you remember, and what you think you remember, the editions and redactions of memory, the corrections and amendations and blundered readings and the whole *apparatus criticus* of the conscious mind trying to make bread out of soup. The way I remember it, I bashed Its head against something until It screamed, then I tried strangling It, then I broke Its arms and legs, and then I bashed It some more. All impossible, I now realize, since They don't have arms, legs, heads, so whatever I did to It could only have been equivalents. But whatever I did, I hurt It, and it was fun.

I have no way of knowing, of course, how long we were cooped up in there together. My best guess, based on what my mother told me (about recurring nightmares she'd had, that sort of thing), is something between three and four months; but, what the hell, time is subjective, especially between us and Them. We were in there together for a long time, and then I was born and It was able to crawl out and escape, at desperate cost to Itself, but better than staying in there with me. By all accounts, I was a fairly ordinary baby after that, though inclined to be willful.

～

So, we went to see the Duchess. But we couldn't; not even the chaplain. Master Prosper was in there, they told us, with the royal midwife, two nurses, and Master Prosper's authorized biographer (he had two of them working twelve-hour shifts), and nobody could go in until it was all over, not even the Duke. Especially the Duke. I showed them my certificate. They went all thoughtful—it's a really good certificate—but apparently the penalty for disobeying Master Prosper's slightest whim was death by garrotting, so clearly nothing could be done.

They parked the chaplain and me in a small anteroom,

empty except for one straight-backed ivory chair. I sat in it.

"Can you really predict what—?"

I nodded. "In this instance, yes."

"But I thought—"

I turned and looked at him, my full professional look. Someone once explained to me why it's so terrifying. He told me: just for a moment, you get the impression that you can see some of the things those eyes have seen, like a sort of trick mirror. I hope he was exaggerating.

"Sorry," he said.

"That's all right." He'd made me feel guilty. "In this instance, I'm pretty sure."

"Would you care to—?"

I shrugged. "Why the hell not?" I said. And I told him; about waking up next to the dead girl. He went a funny sort of gray color. "It made you do that?"

"While I was asleep," I said. "I know it was Him."

"How can you—?"

"Not the first time," I said. "Not by a long chalk. And the last time this one did something like that—no, I tell a lie, time before that—I was out of action for months, dodging the dead girl's family and the law and all that sort of thing. During which time He was free to get up to all sorts of mischief without having to look over His shoulder every five minutes in case I was sneaking up on Him.

So I thought: If I were Him, what would I be up to, that would justify pulling a prank like that? Bearing in mind what I'm going to do to him when I do catch up with him. Which won't be pretty, believe me." I smiled. I don't think it was a happy smile. "And then I glanced through the *Court Circular,* and the question kind of answered it-self."

Years ago, I came across a man lying in the road. He'd been run over by one of those gigantic carts they use for shipping oak trees down from the forest to the ship-yards, and his back was broken. He was still alive but completely paralyzed, and he had much the same look on his face as my unfortunate friend the chaplain had after I'd explained the position to him. "You think—?"

"Yes," I said. "I think, because I think like He does."

"Dear God."

I grinned. "Oh, we're quite alike in many ways," I said. "In fact, there's only two differences between us that really matter. One, I'm stronger than He is. Much, much stronger."

For some reason, this didn't seem to set the chaplain's mind at rest. Rather the reverse.

"The other," I went on, "is that one day I'll die, but not Him. They can't die. He can hurt—trust me, I know, He can suffer more pain than you could possibly imagine—but He can't die. It's a sort of equilibrium,"

I explained. "Two very different things but nonetheless equivalent."

I'd lost him; not that it signified. "But if you're right," he said, "if that *thing* has got inside—"

Through the closed door we heard that unmistakable sound, a newborn baby's first scream. The chaplain shuddered as though he'd just been stabbed, by his mother.

"Surely there must be something I can do?"

I shook my head. "Not a lot, no."

"But—" Poor sod. Windows of understanding were opening in his mind, but through them poured something that wasn't really light. "Master Prosper—"

I nodded. "He's smart," I said. "Not Master Prosper. Him. He'll have known all about that, you can bet your life."

"The experiment. The philosopher-king. There must be *something*—"

I breathed out slowly, as though I'd just put down a very heavy weight. "Master Prosper," I told him, "doesn't believe in demonic possession. He thinks it's just superstition. In his view, the Invincible Sun is a ball of burning gas floating an incomprehensible distance over our heads, and demons are how we account for the symptoms and effects of various disorders and diseases, entirely mechanical in origin, curable with herbs and therapies. I've read his book, and the case he makes out for it is overwhelming. Did you know, he reckons we weren't created on the sixth day? Instead we're the descendants of those furry things from Permia who live in treetops. I was entirely convinced, until I remembered it isn't actually true. Anyhow, we haven't got a hope in hell of persuading Master Prosper to let me in there, and right now, his word is law. Which is just as well," I added, "because the only possible thing I could do to make things a bit better and avoid the disasters that must inevitably follow would be to kill the baby."

He stared at me, opened his mouth, closed it again. I think people hate me the most when they realize I'm right.

"Which I'd do," I went on, "easy as breathing, because I'd have to. But it wouldn't make me very popular with the Duke, and like I mentioned just now, I'm mortal. And while I can't feel nearly so much pain as He can, I can still feel rather a lot. Hence just as well. For me, anyhow."

I felt sorry for the chaplain, and I'm not the most sympathetic person you'll ever meet. So, yes, I felt guilty. I don't cause the problem, but I'm definitely part of it. Between 55 and 60 percent, I'd say.

"What should we do?" he asked me.

I made a show of thinking about that. "You," I said, "are going to arrange for a transfer, to a post a very, very long way away from here. It may mean less money and less status, but believe me, it'll be worth it."

He stared at me with those dead fish eyes, then nodded. "You?"

"I don't know," I said. "But I'll think of something."

~

Think of something. Think like Him. What would He do?

I didn't have a happy childhood. My parents were prosperous, good people and loved me very much, but I was a miserable, spiteful child, given to picking fights with kids who were bigger and stronger than me, and getting beaten bloody by them. They asked me: Why do you do it, it makes no sense, you know you can't beat us, we're bigger than you are? Why don't you pick on someone your own size—or, better still, someone smaller?

I couldn't tell them they'd completely missed the point, obviously. So I carried on baiting them, and they carried on beating me up and feeling sorry for me, and if it ever occurred to me to wonder why I needed to do these stupid things, I simply assumed that it was just one more of the many simple and obvious things that I didn't know yet, but would in the fullness of time. Meanwhile, I just *knew*, without being able to explain or show my working. After all, you don't ask *why* the square on the hypotenuse is equal to the sum of the squares of the other two sides. It just is.

Then one day one of the bigger boys got sick. His friends went to see him and came away horrified. Half the time, they said, he was yelling and screaming and thrashing about, and the rest of the time he just sat there, as if he were dead or something. It was a while before I could visit him, because he'd beaten me up so badly I was confined to bed; but when I felt strong enough I sneaked out of our house and sneaked into his. I wanted to see him suffering, because he'd hurt me.

I crawled in through a window. His parents had strapped him down tight on a stretcher, for his own good, because they loved him. I stood over him. His eyes were tight shut. I said his name. He opened his eyes and looked at me.

"Oh, for crying out loud," He said. "You again."

For a moment I was confused; then I realized. I realized that I could see Him. Him, the enemy inside my enemy: the cat, the prey. Of course, I knew a tiny bit about it, demonic possession—the tiny bit that everyone knows, of which 90 percent is garbage. "I can see you," I said.

It, no, He grinned at me. *Small world.*

I could hear Him inside my head. "You shouldn't be in there," I said aloud. "Is it you hurting my friend?"

Not your friend. He smashed your face in. He really did

you over. The enemy of my enemy is my friend, right?

"That's like saying the cat's cat is a dog. You shouldn't be in there."

Poor devil, He must have thought it's just a kid, I'll risk it. *So what? What are you going to do about it?*

I showed him. And, being very young and clumsy and inexperienced and uneducated, and not knowing my own strength—well. Fortunately, nobody could ever prove that I'd been in that room; and even if they could have, they'd have had a devil of a job explaining how a nine-year-old child could have done that much damage, even when the victim was strapped to a board.

~

They calculate (probably the same bunch of scholarly know-it-alls who came up with the figure 72,936) that in a botched extraction, whatever the host feels, the demon feels it ten times as much. Based on my experience, I'd say that's roughly accurate. But they don't die, and we do. As I said: equilibrium.

What would He do? Well, I knew the answer to that. He wouldn't bother.

It's a lie to say They're incapable of compassion, because self-pity is still pity, and they're red-hot on that. But put Themselves out to rescue someone else, an individual, a country, a whole region? Forget it. But suppose They *had* to; a direct order from whatever passes among Them as a hierarchy, authority, chain of command? No idea if They've got one, but for the sake of argument.

I had one ally, but useless and busy packing his books and vestments for a long sea voyage. I needed another ally, but all I had to choose from was enemies. So? Story of my life.

When you're making something, you don't choose the tools you use because you like them, because they're your particular friends. You choose the ones that will be most useful. Well, then. That's what He'd do.

~

Modesty, said Master Prosper (speaking slowly, so his duty biographer could take dictation) is simply saying about yourself what other people think about you, and therefore preventing them from saying it out loud. It's certainly a shortcoming of which Master Prosper was entirely innocent. And what he loved above all other things was being right.

Not merely having people acknowledge that he's right; because they may be wrong, more than likely in fact, because everyone else is so dumb. No, it doesn't satisfy him unless he believes it himself. So, in order to get Master

Prosper to like me, I had to give him an opportunity to prove that he was right and I was wrong, deluded, an idiot. Easy peasy.

My friend the chaplain had left me with a letter of introduction addressed to the chamberlain asking if he'd be so kind as to introduce a certain favorite cousin of his to Master Prosper. Said cousin had long been a fanatical admirer of the great man's work, et cetera, and if it was remotely possible that the Master might be induced to spare him a few moments of his inexpressibly precious time—

My guess is that the chaplain had something really good—not just the standard palace dirt but something so rank, you'd need gloves and a mask just to think about it—on the chamberlain, because the very next day I got my papers—full pass, permission to enter the royal apartments at will, all manner of rich and wonderful things, together with a note from Master Prosper's deputy assistant junior secretary stating that the most brilliant man who ever lived would be pleased to receive me in such and such a room at such and such a time. Friends in high places, I said to myself. Sometimes I'm so stupid, I'm amazed I manage to breathe.

～

I was prepared for a fat man in the same way that someone who has grown up on the shores of a five-acre inland
lake is prepared for the sea. There was a *lot* of Master
Prosper. Quite how much of it was necessary, I wouldn't
care to say; maybe 60 percent, which was roughly the ra-
tio of genius to bullshit that made up his mental and spir-
itual being, so probably about that.

Sixty percent of Master Prosper would have been a
tall, handsome, imposing man, with a perfectly bald head
of prodigious size, and a high, pleasant voice, and hands
like a girl. You could tell he was an artist by the way
he'd had the room composed, right down to moving the
windows (I could see the new plaster) so that he'd be
perfectly lit, sitting in his marvelous gold and ebony
throne—his own work, and uncharacteristically actually
almost finished—to receive disciples and worshippers in
the late morning and early evening. It was a big room,
forty feet square, and apart from the great man and the
great man's chair, all it contained was a low, three-legged
stool. I could see why. Anything more would have been
clutter.

The chamberlain had told me, whatever you do, look
him straight in the eye; he can't be doing with toadies
and flatterers, only sincere admirers. And what an eye it
was: small, clear, bright blue, and singular, its twin having been lost to an exploding flask during some excep-

tionally important chemical experiment. In its place was a ball of clear glass, transparent and slightly magnifying. I could see how that would be an asset in the course of abstruse philosophical debate. Catch sight of it when you aren't absolutely prepared, and your mind goes instantly blank.

(Mine did. Tell you why later.)

He smiled at me. People don't usually do that. "You wanted to talk to me."

I nodded. "I want to ask you something."

"Ask away."

"What do you believe," I said, "is the greatest force for good in the whole world?"

He thought about it for nearly a whole half heartbeat. "Art," he said.

"Really?"

"Yes."

Well, I thought, that didn't take long. "Could you possibly explain why you think that?"

He nodded graciously. "Because art," he said, "is beauty, and beauty is the essence of goodness made visible or audible. When you look at a beautiful statue or listen to beautiful music, you are looking at and listening to beauty, which is goodness itself, a force no human can withstand for very long. Therefore, by creating beauty, the artist opens doors and windows in the human mind through which goodness can come flooding in. What we call evil is simply darkness, the absence of light. Light dispels darkness; goodness dispels evil. Beauty dispels evil. Therefore art is the greatest force for good in the whole world."

I nodded. Then I said, "Excuse me, but that's bullshit."

He grinned at me. "Yes," he said. "And no. What I just told you is essentially true, but only under ideal conditions. And conditions are so very rarely ideal."

"For example?"

"If you see light through a glass or a raindrop, the light can be distorted. There's a saying, beauty is in the eye of the beholder. Actually, that's wrong. Beauty is absolute, but the eye of the beholder"—he closed his good eye, leaving the glass monstrosity staring straight at me—"is capable of weakening or corrupting it. If you pass light through a raindrop, you break it up into its component parts. If you pass beauty through the eye of an imperfect beholder, you may get nothing; just canvas daubed with oil, or a piece of stone, or the noise made by blowing down a tube with holes in it. Also," he added, "the art may not be particularly good art."

"Ah," I said.

"To counter which," he went on, "we must train the eye, so that the beholder beholds correctly. And we must make good art. When we've done that, art can be the greatest force for good in the world."

"Excuse me," I said. "I said *is*, not *can be*."

He laughed. "But you used the superlative, *greatest*. There are other forces for good, and very strong some of them may be, but you asked for the greatest, and I answered the question you asked. I was also generous enough to point out certain conditions and qualifications, which I needn't have done, strictly speaking."

"I see," I said. "And so you create art to make the world better."

Tiny nod. "And for money," he said, and paused; and when I didn't laugh, continued, "but mostly to open windows in dark places. Such as this."

"You have a project in hand?"

Bigger nod. "The Duke has commissioned me," he said, "to cast for him a great bronze statue to be set up in the parade grounds out there beyond the palace. I have agreed. I shall cast a statue of a colossal bronze horse. It will be my lesser masterpiece."

"Ah yes," I said. "After the child."

I'd said the right thing. "Art is the greatest force for good, but only under the right conditions. Second greatest is the creation of a truly wise and good king. Under the conditions prevailing, the second best is more likely to have more effect more quickly. Once the land is ruled by a truly wise and good king, the conditions necessary for the greatest force to be effective will be established."

That was all right, then. "Thank you," I said.

"I've answered your question?"

"Perfectly. Now I know."

"Knowledge is everything."

"Thank you. I'll go now."

It took me all my strength and determination to back out of the room. As I left, pausing on the threshold to wipe sweat out of my eyes, I glanced at the great man's face. He was white as a sheet.

~

Let me inside your head for a moment. You're thinking: Something is wrong here. That was supposed to be a true record of a debate between—well, yes, some nonentity on the one hand, but on the other, the greatest genius who ever lived. So, either the record is accurate and Prosper of Schanz was just an egotistical fat man, or the narrative is in error, and (come to think of it) we have only this clown's word that he ever met Prosper—

There is, of course, a perfectly reasonable explanation. You try holding two conversations simultaneously, and see how you like it.

It came as a shock, now I think of it, to meet a new face after so many years in the business. When I say *face*—

I don't know you, I said.

She—I'll come back to that in a minute—She looked at me as though I was unimportant but mildly interesting. *I don't suppose you do,* she said.

Of course, I said, *I wouldn't. You're from Schanz, presumably.*

A smile, faintly patronizing but so what? *Falhoel, actually. But well outside your territory. Where I'm originally from, you really don't want to know.*

Of course, I said, and realized I'd repeated myself. *He lived in Falhoel for a while.*

Published Principles of Mathematics *there. And that's where I picked him up.*

And that's why he hasn't published since?

She sort of twinkled at me; smart, She didn't need to say, I like a boy with spirit. *I picked him up before he wrote* Principles.

Ah.

Why *She*? To which I can only say, you had to be there. She looked like—well, maybe they all look like that in Falhoel; in which case, I definitely got a raw deal when the territories were apportioned. I doubt it, though. And why on earth should I be surprised? We—humans—aren't all the same. Some of us look and talk and act like gods and goddesses; some of us look and talk and act like pigs. Just that on my patch, I'd only ever encountered pigs.

But so what? That's no more than the difference between Downtown and Old Town, after all.

Now, then, She said. *You're not going to be difficult, are you?*

I thought about it. *I have a duty.*

She yawned. *Yes, of course you do. And if you insist, I'll leave.*

And take half his brains with you?

More than half. She twinkled again. *Say about sixty percent. And wouldn't that be a loss to the human race?*

Prosper of Schanz, the greatest, et cetera. *Yes,* I said.

Well, then. Or you could leave me in peace. It's not like I'm doing anyone any harm, after all.

I thought about that too. *You must be,* I said. *You have a duty.*

Oh, well, in the very long term, obviously, yes. Her voice was like honey; the sweet-scented honey, where the bees suck on lavender. *There's a grand design, in which he plays a part. But it's very big. It's so big you have to stand a long way back to see it. Close up, what harm am I doing? Quite the reverse, actually.*

I had to ask. *Everything he's ever done, everything he's achieved. That was all—?*

Oh, not everything. Just the best bits. At a rough guess, I'd say sixty percent.

Not just the paintings and the sculptures (though I

had it on the very best authority that art is the greatest force for good in the world). The science, the medicine, the engineering; so little of which he'd so far published—

And which would all be lost, She broke in, *if I had to pack my bags and go. But if I stay—*

He'll start finishing things.

That made Her giggle. *You could put it like that, yes. No promises, mind. But why not?*

I frowned. *Why should you? What about your duty?*

Tut-tut. Silly me. I think Saloninus puts it so well—

And oftentimes, to bring us to our harm,
The instruments of darkness tell us truths

—which, She went on, *is only the half of it. It's so easy to think in black-and-white all the time, either I win or you do. But it's so much easier and better if we both win. One of us more than the other, maybe, but both of us, definitely. Can't you see the sense in that? No, I don't suppose you can.*

I felt hurt. *Sure,* I said. *Like a joint venture. We get something out of it, so do you. No, come to think of it, I can't imagine that. You and us, collaborating—*

Sigh. Oh, why not? Just think. Open your mind, just for once. Imagine a man, a single man who contributes more to his species than anyone else, ever. The whole world made bright and glorious by his genius, his ideas—

Which you put in his head.

Not entirely. Sixty percent. Well, maybe sixty-five. Yes, She said, *and what's wrong with that, for pity's sake? Like that saying you have: his money's as good as yours. The ideas are pure gold. Well, aren't they?*

Principles of Mathematics. And *Madonna of the Oak Trees.* And the Ninth Symphony. And why should the angels have all the best tunes? *There's got to be something in it for you,* I said.

Twinkle. *Of course there is. But, like I told you, it's the big picture. So big, it probably won't even start working out and coming good in your lifetime. So—not your problem, not your fault. Or would you rather be remembered as the man who murdered Prosper of Schanz?*

I'd always hated all of Them, on sight, instinctively. But not all of Them are alike. The same level of difference as between, say, me and Master Prosper.

This whole thing, I said, *was your idea.*

By "this whole thing," you mean—

The philosopher-king. The perfect society.

Oh, that. No, that wasn't me. That's the grand design. Well, a part of it.

Sixty per—?

Much smaller. Say five. That's one of the good things about not having to die, you can plan for the long term. On the other hand, you do have to be accountable for your mistakes.

You've got to face the music, you can't just cheerfully die before you're found out.

Your grand design, I said. *I could stop it.*

She thought about it. *Stop it,* She said, *probably not. Derail it, divert it, make it take some other shape entirely—well, maybe you could and maybe you couldn't. But don't quote me on that.*

Your grand design.

Yes. But, stop and think, will you?

What on earth could there possibly be to think about?

—At which point I heard myself talking to someone.

"I've answered your question?"

"Perfectly. Now I know."

"Knowledge is everything."

—and I knew the audience was over. She couldn't get rid of me, but Prosper could. It all comes down to who's stronger, after all.

Knowledge is everything? Bullshit. Besides, it's not what you know—

Their grand design. Think about it, as They would.

They can think long-term much more easily than we can. So, long-term, what would be the worst damage They could do with the ingredients currently under Their control?

The trouble is, you can't always think like Them, just as you can't walk up a wall like a spider, even though you have legs too. Different sort of legs. So, if it were me, designing the grand design—

Easy peasy. Here's a child with all the advantages—monarch of all he surveys, which is always a good place to start from, and also educated by the great man himself, the greatest man ever, who's taught him *everything he knows.* And no secret has been made of this; everyone knows that this kid is destined to be the Superman, the ultimate human being. Absolute power, backed up by absolute and universal goodwill. Just think what the instruments of darkness could do with that.

Just think; not as we think, we mortals, we mayflies. Instead, think as *They* think, aiming for a bigger, better result a hundred years from now, five hundred years, a thousand years, five thousand. And in the meantime, five thousand years of meantime, while their grand design is working itself out . . . Cities will rise and fall, civilizations. Dust and grass and sand will cover all of us, all our achievements, apart from those of Master Prosper, whose work will survive in translations of translations of translations, while our bones and stones will lie forgotten in the wet earth, unless the plow turns them up, and scholars will puzzle themselves to death trying to decipher our work. And still the grand design won't be complete, the hammer won't have fallen, the snare won't have tightened round the ankle of poor stupid mayfly humanity; so that, when it does, who the hell will there be to connect cause to effect?

But I could stop it. And the price we'd all have to pay would be the life and work of Prosper of Schanz. I ask you, what would you do?

~

What would *He* do?

(All my life, I've met so many people, but for me there's only ever one *Him.*) Why would I ask myself a question like that? I'd known Him all my life, so I knew (among other things) that He wasn't exactly bright, certainly not a towering genius like Master Prosper. But I knew Him so well I knew His finer qualities.

Oh, They have them, for sure. It's a bizarre but widespread myth that only heroes have good qualities, and the only qualities heroes have are good; villains are, by definition, all bad. Bullshit.

Think about it. Think of the qualities it takes to be a successful or even a competent criminal. You need courage—to climb into a stranger's house, the floor plan of which you don't know, fully aware that the householder is almost certainly well provided with weapons, large dogs, strong and active servants—would *you* want to do that?—and for what? A sackful of small, portable artworks, for which you'll probably get ten groschen on the kreutzer. To which add a calm, deliberate mind, resourcefulness, a steady hand, a delicate touch, the ability to work quickly and methodically. And that's just your scum-of-the-earth, back-alley burglar. Take the truly dreadful, evil men of history, slaughterers of nations in the name of some twisted ideal. Of necessity you must allow them to have had Faith (which moves mountains, and without which mere works are in vain) and Hope, Loyalty, and Self-Sacrifice in the Name of the Cause, and practically every other noble and glorious characteristic you can possibly think of, except for the small matter of being in the right. . . .

(Which—the older I get, the more convinced I am—is just fashion anyhow, like the brims on hats or the trimming of ladies' sleeves. And if you don't believe me, just think how much morality has changed—in your lifetime—and then read a little history and ask yourself: Do you really, honestly think these changes will be *permanent*?)

So, He has finer qualities. He knows, instinctively, what's worth suffering pain for, and what isn't. He knows when to leave quickly and gracefully, and when to stick around and be torn out by the roots. In judging whether the game is worth the candle, He knows the price of candles better than anyone else I ever met.

It's not something you tell people about, obviously. Not your parents, not your friends, not your dear old uncle or your favorite aunt: *I can see the devil in people. I can see the devil in you.* And, when you're just a kid, you don't know the rules, what's expected, what is and isn't done, and there's nobody to ask, and you're scared. But you keep on seeing the cat, out of the corner of your eye, and it becomes unbearable not to bark, chase, bite.

Maybe I was different; maybe I'm just a thoroughly bad person, with loads of bad, wicked qualities, such as wanting to bark and liking to bite. Whatever. I managed to keep myself on the leash until I met Him again, in the eyes of my enemy, and that was it, all my self-possession used up. From then on, I was out of control. If I saw one of Them, I went for the throat, and that was that.

We had to move; several times; a lot. Sometimes it was because of all the desperate people crowding round our door, begging, imploring—heal me, make my son better, please cure my mother, she's going to die—and nothing I could do, because it wasn't Them, it was consumption or fever or all the thousands of things that tear you up and kill you that aren't Them. And sometimes it was because It wouldn't go quietly, or reckoned I was only a kid and could be messed with, and you can guess by now how that ended.

Word gets around. They—the other *they,* the good

guys—tracked me down and took me away, and taught me to be a better dog; faster, neater, slicker, deadlier. They told me: in all our years of doing this, we've never found one quite like you. Quite a few of them said that to me, but none of them cared to explain exactly what they meant by it.

Ours is a small, select order. We don't have hierarchies, endowments, liturgies, orthodoxies, prebendaries, cathedrals. We aren't exactly popular or fashionable. Kings don't give us vast estates, people don't leave us money in their wills, we don't have handsome vestments or valuable silverware; just authority. But what we lack in wealth and the younger sons of the nobility we make up for in efficiency. And we do have respect. Nothing clears a crowded street faster than one of us.

We don't have a hierarchy, but we can't help having the occasional dog who's even bigger, faster, nastier than the other big, fast, nasty dogs. Nobody wants to be like that—another thing we don't have is ambition, that'd be like pushing and shoving to get to the front of the queue for the gallows—but it happens. It happened to me, and I owe it all to—

~

You again.

I smiled. *Me.*

I was younger then, of course. Twenty-three, and four years a qualified professional. Cocky as hell and enjoying myself.

Look, He said. *This is stupid. You can't keep picking on me like this. It's unreasonable.*

(Curious thing: As I grew older, more articulate, better educated, so did He. First few times we met, He talked in grunts. But when I started reading books and going to lectures, He started using long words and complex syntax. Would you care to speculate about how that happened? I can't be bothered.)

Fuck unreasonable, I said. *Get out. Now.*

Also, I couldn't help noticing, He was getting smarter. More sophisticated, let's say. Impossible, because He was thousands or millions of years old when I was born, so it wasn't as though we were growing up together. But definitely more cunning. *Sure,* He said. *If you really want me to.*

The host this time was, believe it or not, the public executioner for the southeastern district of Elagaba Province. He'd been acting funny, people said, for a long time. One day he'd be happy as birds in springtime, whistling, smiling, taking his hat off to ladies in the street. Next day, you'd find him sitting in the dark somewhere, head in hands, crying his eyes out. And the effect on his work—it's quite a skilled business, they told me, there's far more to it than people realize. You need to be able to figure out the length of drop based on the individual's height and weight. You need to judge angles and the precise degree of power to sever the spinal cord. Otherwise, you get people's heads coming off when they're hanged, and not coming off when they're beheaded, and that sort of thing reflects on the community as a whole.

You can pull me out, if you really want to, He said. *You know you can.*

I looked a little bit closer, and got that shivery feeling. Sophisticated; He must have been in there quite some time before it started to show, because He'd sort of expanded into all the tendrils and nerve endings, like grass growing up through netting. Sure, I could pull Him out, but—

You've been busy, I said.

I'll be straight with you, He said. *I've had a rough time of it the last few years. Every time I've got anything settled, one of you bastards comes and moves me on, and every one of you was rough. There's such a thing as proportionate use of force, you know. Or wasn't that on the syllabus where you were?*

I was away sick that day.

What I need, He said reproachfully, *is somewhere I can rest up, just for a bit, long enough to get myself back together, in one piece.*

What you need, I said, *is to get out of there right now.*

Oh, come on, He said. *Be reasonable, for once in your life. I'm not doing any real harm in here. All right, sometimes he's dead miserable, but sometimes he's really happy. It's not like he's biting people or bashing his head against walls.*

I grinned. *You're interfering with his duties.*

Yes, sure. People aren't getting killed on time, and what an appalling state of affairs that must be. You do realize, most of the people he'd have killed, but for me, are completely innocent.

Most?

He sort of shrugged. *Roughly sixty percent. That's innocent lives prolonged, because of me. That's a good thing, surely? Anyway, here's the deal: You go away and come back in six months, and I promise faithfully, I'll undo all my clever little knots and unpick my stitches and I'll go quiet as a lamb, and not a mark on him. Or you can force me out now, and what's left of his brain will leak out of his ears like honey. Up to you.*

I shook my head. *You're bluffing,* I told Him. *You're playing me for an idiot. I know you. If I leave you in there, you'll just intertwine your way deeper and deeper inside.*

No, I promise. Word of honor.

Have you any idea, I told Him, *how much I could hurt you, getting you out of there by force?*

He took a moment to answer. *Actually, yes.*

And are you asking me to believe that you'd risk that, just to play games with me?

There was a sort of artful gleam about Him, though He tried to hide it. *It's not about how much it hurts me, surely,* He said. *It's how much it hurts* him.

I smiled at Him. *Can't let the likes of you get away with anything,* I said. *Bad precedent. Rule One, we don't negotiate with the instruments of darkness. If the host is injured, that's very regrettable, but it's entirely your fault, not ours.*

I told you, He said, and for all I know, His distress was genuine; for all I care. *Word of honor, I said, didn't I? We can't break our word, you know that. Don't you? Didn't they teach you that at wizard school?*

They taught me Rule One, I said. *No negotiating. Besides, you think you've been really clever, but you're stupid. I can have you out of there with a flick of the wrist, and hardly any damage to speak of. To him,* I added. *Not to you.*

Sorry, I didn't quite catch that. Which of us did you say was bluffing?

I don't appreciate being spoken to like that, not by one of Them, not by Him. Besides, I honestly believed I could do it, without too much friendly harm. We all make honest mistakes sometimes, even the best of us.

Just as well that nobody really likes public executioners, even though they do a necessary job that nobody else is prepared to do. And word gets about. It must have been a colossal, titanic struggle, people said (even among my own order, who should know better; should have known me better), or it wouldn't have made such a godawful mess of a battlefield. And anyone capable of winning a battle that did so much damage must be—well. *A real piece of work,* I think was the term they used. Meant kindly, I'm sure.

~

She sent for me.

For Her, of course, I wouldn't have gone. For Master Prosper, I had no choice. I could have refused, theoretically; in which case, a range of options, from being thrown out of the Duchy to being dragged into the palace by my heels. I gather schoolmasters have a saying when they're about to thrash some poor kid within an inch of his life: this will hurt me more than it hurts you. Bullshit.

Master Prosper received me in the Alabaster Room, which he'd taken over and converted into a drawing office, studio, and workshop. The end wall had been whitewashed—covering a thousand-year-old fresco of the *Ascension of the Invincible Sun*—and on it, the great man had sketched out in charcoal, actual size, the seven components of the great bronze horse. He was standing on a ladder with the charcoal in his hand, motionless, when I was shown in. He turned his head and smiled at me.

"We were talking," he said, "about the power of art to do good."

"I remember."

"This—" He waggled the stick of charcoal. "—will be my masterpiece. What do you think?"

When all else fails, tell the truth. "Magnificent," I said.

He backed down the ladder, feeling for the rungs with his toes. "As a work of art," he said, "and as a piece of engineering. Nothing—nothing—on this scale has ever been attempted before."

"Is that right?"

He laughed. "Take my word for it," he said, "as an engineer."

The Alabaster Room is where they used to hold state banquets and receptions for really important ambassadors. The end wall is vast. It was only just big enough. "I suppose it won't be easy," I said, "casting something that big."

"You could say that." He sat down, waved to me to do the same. "One hundred and forty tons of bronze." He smiled at me once more. "If I tried to cast it in one piece, the sheer weight of the liquid metal would burst the mold, unless I made a mold the size of a mountain, which in turn would crush the wax core inside it as it was built up. But if I make it in pieces, how do I put the pieces together? And consider this: Molten metal cools from the outside, while the inside remains hot, and as it cools it shrinks. With an ordinary statue, say life-size, it hardly matters, but on a scale like this, the force of the contraction will shatter the casting. There's a reason—many reasons—why nobody has ever made a statue this big before. Quite simply, it can't be done."

He paused. I think I was supposed to say something, but I didn't.

"The statue," he said, "will be my present to the young Prince. It will be unveiled on the day of his baptism, two months from now."

"That doesn't leave you very much—"

"Can't be done." He grinned at me. "Simply bringing about the golden age isn't enough. People have to be convinced, or they won't believe. They need miracles. My job is to provide them. Simple as that."

I nodded blankly. "Was there something?" I said.

"What?"

"You sent for me."

He gave me a mild frown. "You were interested," he said. "In beauty and the power of art."

He had a point there. I'd forgotten. "Naturally," I said. "But you're a very busy man. I didn't imagine you could spare the time to talk to someone like me. Not unless there was something I could do for you."

He paused again, looking at me as though deciding how best to cut me into sections, for ease of remanufacture (in his image, presumably). "You didn't come here to ask me a facile, pointless question, of no possible relevance to yourself."

"No."

"I know who you are. I know what you do. You know I don't believe in any of it."

I dipped my head slightly in acknowledgment. One must be polite.

"Do you suspect that I . . . ?"

He didn't finish the sentence. Big surprise. The one thing everybody knows about Master Prosper, he never finishes anything. Why should he? Completions are for assistants and apprentices; genius needs only to make the incredible, inspired start.

"It did cross my mind," I said.

He looked at me. Or at least, part of him did. At a rough guess, say 40 percent. "And?" he said.

"Excuse me?"

It hit me like a fist in the mouth. Forty percent of him was very scared indeed. "You wouldn't have come here, gone to all this trouble, if you didn't have reason to believe— Well?"

"I'm sorry," I said. "I don't understand. You're a skeptic. You think it's all garbage."

"Am I or am I not?"

I counted to three under my breath, and said, "No."

He closed his eyes, just for a moment. Then he leaned back in his Imperial chair and he wept.

And while he was preoccupied, I looked past him. *I know you're in there,* I said.

No answer.

Was that entirely necessary? I asked.

Playing games. So I reached in—taking very great care that the cuff of my sleeve didn't brush against anything, like the curator of the Imperial porcelain, or the Imperial scorpion collection—and prodded very gently. She bit me.

That's rude, She said.

What was all that in aid of?

Twinkle. *He's smart,* She said. *He's been thinking. It's gradually starting to dawn on him that he couldn't have done all that clever stuff on his own. Of course, if it hadn't been for me, he'd never have been smart enough to get that far, but that's the thanks you get for helping. So, anyway, you've just set his mind at rest. Thank you.*

If I'd told him the truth—

She sighed. *I'd have had to kill him and then I'd have had the whole tedious job to do all over again, with someone else. Setting the grand design back a hundred years, and depriving humanity of its homegrown god. Not to mention the bronze horse, which is going to be gorgeous, trust me. Though I don't suppose you like art.*

Not much, no.

Barbarian. She sighed. *I'm going to let him make his horse,* She said. *In fact, I'm going to encourage him, and tell him how to do it. Not because it's part of the grand design, or at least it's only a tiny peripheral part, and something far more mundane would do just as well. Simply for the joy of it. You know—a thing of beauty and a joy forever. Something I can point to, a thousand years from now, and say, I did that. Just because it's beautiful.*

I was sick and tired of the sight of Her. *It can't be done,* I told Her. *Not without magic, at any rate.*

No such thing as magic. You should know that, better than anyone.

Delighted to hear it. In that case, it can't be done. He knows why. Ask him.

He's a smart boy. She sounded like a proud mother. *He'll think of something.*

~

There's smart, and there's smart *enough.*

I went away and did some reading in the Temple library; starting (of course) with *Principles of Mathematics* and moving onward and outward—Numerian, Otkel the Stammerer, Saloninus on the properties of materials, Carnifex's *Mirror of Various Arts.* They confirmed what I already vaguely knew and what Master Prosper himself had told me. Couldn't be done.

There are limits, said the consensus of a thousand years of learning and research. They may seem arbitrary—they are arbitrary—but there are limits to what you can do with wax and clay and molten bronze. Even if you were a giant, twenty feet tall, strong enough to pick up small islands one-handed, there would still be limits. These limits were thoroughly tested by Aimo of Boll, seven hundred years ago; he was commissioned by the Emperor to make the biggest possible bronze statue of his eldest son, who had just died of venereal disease at the age of twenty. Expense no object; the full resources of the Empire at his beck and whim. So Aimo started with the biggest statue he thought he could get away with, and that worked just fine; then he made one 5 percent bigger, and that was fine; the next one 5 percent bigger still, and so on. As he progressed, he figured out a series of the most amazingly ingenious fixes, work-arounds, and cheats to cope with various insuperable problems as they arose, learning whole bookfuls of valuable, undreamed-of new stuff about breaking strains and shearing forces and sectional densities and tensile strengths with each successful augmentation, until eventually he reached the point when there were no more fixes, work-arounds, or cheats (like a man on a rock in the middle of the sea, finding he's run out of higher ground to retreat to) and declared, for all time: this is as far as you can go, and no further. And then he set to with his logarithmic tables and his abacus and figured out the ratios and wrote them down; and when I read them, I understood why Master Prosper had arrived at the dimensions of his Great Horse. Aimo's maxima, plus 5 percent.

~

He was too busy to see me, so I wrote him a letter. I said: *If you make your Great Horse 5 percent smaller, it'll still be a very big horse indeed, and it'll be possible.* I didn't expect a reply but I got one. A single word: *Exactly.* And a postscript: *Come and see me, anytime you like.*

Valid point. For a man like Prosper of Schanz, if something's possible, why bother doing it?

Fine. But, for reasons of my own—

Why have you suddenly decided to help me? She said.

I shrugged. *You convinced me. Well, he convinced me. Both of you together. You're right, of course.*

Are we?

I nodded. *I think so. It's a matter of perspective.*

Perspective.

Ask him about it, he's an artist. It's about what's close, what's a very long way away, and all the stuff in between. Also the old saying about birds in hands and bushes.

I'm not sure I follow.

That's because you're not very good at taking yes for an answer. All right. Granted, I told Her, *that your grand design is undoubtedly something very nasty and bad, eventually, in the long term. But you're immortal and I'm not, so if I stop you now, you'll just wait till I'm dead and start all over again, so really, what's the point in me interfering?*

She gave me the look I deserved. *Immortal, yes. Also, not born yesterday.*

I'm not saying I'm happy about it, I told Her. *Or reconciled to it, even. But I've just read a very interesting book about what is and isn't possible. And stopping you isn't possible. Making life difficult, yes. Stopping, no.*

She didn't say anything. I blundered on, like a blind man on a cliff edge. *I can't see a thousand years into the future,* I told Her, *so I can't see the nasty, evil outcome. What I can see is Master Prosper's horse, which is going to be amazingly beautiful. And thousands and millions of people who haven't even been born yet will look at that horse and hear about how it was made, even though it was impossible, and maybe it'll give them that little extra bit of strength and hope they need to persevere with scrambling up this shit heap we call life. And—I don't know. I really can't imagine what you've got up your sleeve that's so incredibly bad and horrible that Prosper's horse wouldn't have been worth it. From our perspective, I mean.*

Twinkle. *I do believe you've actually been listening to what I've been telling you,* She said.

Don't sound so surprised. After all, we're the same in so many things, it's our differences that matter. The only real difference is duration. And, given that difference, why can't we both win? Since our definitions of what constitutes victory—

Ah! She purred like a cat. *Exactly.*

Short-term and long-term, I said. *Who says a thousand years of enlightened peace isn't worth the inevitable smash that comes after it? We both win.*

Also, She said, *you can't stop me. You already admitted it.*

There is that. And you've never actually won anything. Have you?

She didn't answer that. Sore point.

Like the famous general in the Revolutionary War, I went on tactlessly. *Fought twenty-seven battles, got beaten twenty-seven times. But he won the war. Every time we catch up with you, we stop you and throw you out, and it hurts, and you're back to square one. Guess what,* I said. *I'm not unique. After I'm dead, there'll be another one like me, just as powerful. But he won't be prepared to break Rule One.*

Rule One.

Never negotiate with the enemy.

Oh, that's Rule One. No, I see what you mean. And you would?

Rules are made to be broken, I said. *If it's the right thing to do.*

I'd given Her a lot to think about, and Master Prosper was starting to wake up from his after-dinner snooze. *So,* She said, *you want to help me.*

Yes, I said. *I suppose I do.*

A sort of collaboration. Twinkle twinkle. *No offense,* She said, *but how can you help, exactly? He's a genius. You're—*

Yes, I said. *But there's something that's holding you back that I don't have.*

Really? What?

I gave Her my very, very best grin. *Scruples.*

~

So I went to a foundry, where they showed me how you cast things in bronze.

You start with a slab of beeswax, which looks like stale cheese and smells like honey. You carve the wax, and you warm up bits till they're soft and mold them like clay, and squidge them on until you've got what you want, only made of wax instead of bronze. Then you pack the right sort of fine-grained clay all around the wax and fire it in a kiln to make it hard, like brick; this melts out the wax, and you're left with a hollow mold.

Then you get molten wax and you dribble it into the mold and swirl it round, until the sides of the mold are covered in a thick layer of wax. Then you break the mold—very, very carefully; and guess what, you've now got more or less what you started off with (a wax statue), only it's hollow. This is important, because all bronze statues are hollow, to save expensive metal and horribly inconvenient weight. You fill your hollow wax with a sort of soup made of plaster mixed with fine sand, which sets hard; that's called the core. It's brittle, so when the statue's finished, you can smash it into lumps and powder with a thin metal rod and get it out again. To keep the core from shifting during the casting process, you drive little nails through the wax into the plaster.

Next, you warm up some extra wax and roll it out like pastry into thin rods, which you stick at strategic points to your waxwork. These will be the channels, through which the hot metal will flow in and the displaced air will be pushed out. (That's very important; otherwise, you get air pockets and bubbles, which are disastrous.)

Next, you get a whole lot of *exactly* the right kind of clay and you pack it round the waxwork and very *carefully* round the wax channels, packing it very thick indeed, and then you put it in a kiln and fire it, melting out the wax, leaving you with a hollow brick mold with an inner plaster core pinned to the mold with nails. The gap between the mold and the core is where you pour the bronze, and that'll be your sculpture. Melt a load of scrap bronze in a crucible, being very careful not to let the sweat from your face fall in the melt (water and hot metal, very bad; a small explosion, and your eyes full of white-hot shrapnel); grip the crucible in a pair of long tongs and slowly and carefully pour the bronze into the upside-down mold. Go away for twelve hours, come back, smash the mold, and there's your statue, plus strange-looking ivy growing up it (that's the bronze-filled channels, called runners or sprues), which you cut off with a hacksaw and smooth off with a file. Then a quick rubdown with sharp sand, and you're done.

That's a small statue, something you can lift with one hand; a paperweight. Now imagine doing it with a mold the size of a house.

Master Prosper had mentioned some of the problems—the sheer weight of the metal being too much for the mold, differential cooling. There were others. Shoring up the mold internally, with beams like house rafters, so it wouldn't pull apart under its own weight before it set. Or how about balance? The horse would, of course, be rearing on its hind legs, front legs pawing the air. The weight of the front end would be far more than the back legs could bear; they'd either bend or snap like carrots, unless you had an ugly great, big prop to support the front, off-the-ground end. And how do you lift up, swirl round, and upend a brick as big as the White Feather Temple?

I remember one time when I woke up and found myself surrounded by men I didn't know. Two of them had axes, and one had a sledgehammer. They looked terrified. "Don't try anything," one of them said.

"What's going on?" I said. "Who are you? I don't understand."

They were looking at my hands. I looked at my hands.

"Don't try anything," one of them said. A different one, I think.

They tied my hands behind my back, real tight, then tied my feet together with a rope just shorter than my stride, as people do with horses. Don't try anything, they told me, and led me across the street to the Brother's house.

"Ecclesiastical jurisdiction," the Brother explained, looking slightly past rather than at me. "Technically you have benefit of clergy, so civil authority can't try you."

"What did I do?"

My hands were behind my back, but I'd seen what they looked like. I couldn't remember anything; my memory was soft and raw, like the socket where a tooth's been pulled out. But I guessed I'd done something more than cut myself shaving.

He didn't answer in words. Instead he pulled a sheet off something lying on the table—a girl, about twelve; most of her, anyway. I recognized her. I'd evicted an old acquaintance from her brother three days earlier.

"I plead benefit of clergy," I said.

The Brother gave me a sad look. "I'm a clergyman," he said. "I have jurisdiction."

"Not over my order."

Which was, of course, completely untrue, but did he know that? Turned out he didn't.

"You'll have to write to Headquarters at the White Feather Temple," I told him. "They'll send down a duly accredited arbitrator. It'll take about a month."

That why-does-it-have-to-be-me look—I know it so well. The town council held a brief discussion, which the charcoal merchant lost. He had a cellar, with only one door and no window, only a hatch with bolts on the outside and a padlock. He wasn't happy about it, but what can you do?

One of my colleagues turned up six weeks later. I have no idea what he said to the Brother, but I was back outside in the light before his horse had finished its nosebag.

"You clown," my colleague said, once we were out of town.

"You don't understand," I told him. "There was nothing I could've done. It got inside me while I was asleep. The first thing I knew about it was when they showed me the body."

He didn't answer. At the crossroads, he took the left fork, indicating with his hand that I should take the right.

Four months later, I caught up with my old acquaintance.

You should be dead, He said.

I pulled Him out, but not before I'd given Him a few experiences to remember me by. *We'll meet again,* I told Him, *and by then I'll have thought of something even better. Lots of better things. I'm looking forward to it,* I told him quite truthfully.

It was self-defense, he mumbled when eventually I let him go. *You're always so vicious, I can't stand it anymore. So I tried to get rid of you. And whose fault was that?*

Yours, I told Him. *For existing.*

You haven't heard the last of this.

Almost certainly not.

He's persistent but not imaginative. I'm remorseless and my imagination is prodigious. And so it goes, on and on.

~

The young Prince, Master Prosper told me, was coming along very nicely. Very clever, very clever indeed. A prodigy.

Master Prosper had taken a liking to me. Whenever he had a spare moment, he liked to walk with me in the cloister. Before the first Duke overthrew the old Republic, the palace had been a monastery. At the center was half an acre of herb gardens, with cloisters running round three sides. Partly, he said, he enjoyed my company; it wasn't often that he had a chance to talk to someone whose mind was so little cluttered with education or accepted opinions—

("You mean I'm stupid."

"Good heavens, no. Just ignorant.")

Partly, he confessed, he wanted to have me near him, because he was scared. Not that he believed in that sort of thing. (He had a sort of intellectual integrity, I'll give him that.) He had proved beyond any reasonable doubt that gods and devils were simply myth and superstition, but deep in his unruly peasant heart ("My father was a village apothecary and my mother was a goatherd's daughter. Can you imagine?") he believed. . . . And belief, like love and sleep, is something you can't do anything about. You can't make it come if you want it, and you can't make it go if you don't.

"It's stupid of me," he told me, in a low voice, "but I'm worried. I don't feel *right,* somehow. Recently I feel as though something is trying to peer inside me. Yes, I know. Me, of all people. But having you close to me reassures me. So, indulge an old fool."

"I've been thinking about what you said the other day," I said, a few days later. She was glaring at me but I ignored Her. "This anxious feeling you've been getting."

He laughed. "Oh, that's all right. Superstition. Just my inner goatherd getting above himself."

Many a true word. "Humor me," I said. "I happen to be a professional. Tell me, this feeling. When did you first notice it?"

He frowned. "I don't really know."

"Might it have been," I said, "shortly after the Prince was born?"

He stopped dead and stared at me. He wasn't the only one. She was yelling at me, but I tuned Her out.

"I think it might have been," he said. "You don't think—"

"I try not to theorize without data," I said. "You taught me that."

"But the Prince. A newborn child—"

I shrugged. "Particularly vulnerable," I said. "And incredibly tempting, under the circumstances, if you consider the implications."

He sat down on a window ledge. "But that would be terrible. The worst disaster imaginable."

"Yes."

He looked up at me, the way people do. "If it's true—"

"I could tell you at a glance if it is or not."

"Would there be—? Could you do anything?"

I gave him the customers' smile. "Like I said. I'm a professional."

"But very young children—I understand the dangers are considerable."

"Yes," I said. "But I'm the best there is."

He thought, for a very long time. She was howling and screaming and threatening to stop his pulse or give him a massive stroke. It was fun, watching Her lose Her cool like that. "All you need to do is see the Prince, and you can tell, one way or the other?"

"I need to be ten feet away or closer," I lied, "to be absolutely sure."

"That can be arranged."

"If it'll set your mind at rest," I said. I can be so thoughtful and considerate. "It'll only take a minute."

~

Me again, I said.

Poor soul, He was terrified. *Keep that bastard the hell away from me!* He yelled. I'm not used to Them addressing me in the third person. Then I realized. He was talking to Her.

She didn't seem unduly concerned. *Is that him? The one you told me about, who keeps picking on you?*

That's him, all right. You said—

Did she promise? I asked him. *To protect you from the horrible monster?*

Yes.

After all these years, you still don't know me very well. I grinned at him. *You're safe,* I said. *I can't get you out without hurting the Prince.*

You don't care. You don't give a damn. You never did.

Oh, come on, I said. *You know me better than that.*

I know you. A world of pain and resentment in three little words. *I get it, you're trying to kid—what did you call it,* Her? Pause, while the implications sank in. *You're sick, you know that?*

Why should I bother trying to deceive one of you?

You're capable of anything.

Bless the child, I said, so She could hear me—neat trick, by the way, which to the best of my knowledge none of my order has ever attempted, let alone succeeded. *He doesn't like me. Trying to get me into trouble by pretending I've done bad things. She knows better than that.*

Don't use that word. It's disgusting.

She knows I wouldn't try and pull you out of the Prince, because of the risk. The baby and the bathwater, as the saying goes. I paused, letting him have a nice long soak in my personality. *My job's to save people, not to rip them apart. No, I'm just paying my respects to an old friend, that's all.*

Can't you get him killed or something? he yelled past me, at Her. *Or arrested or banished or something? He's evil. He's a lunatic.*

I sighed. *She's been keeping you out of the loop,* I said. *Didn't She tell you? We're all on the same side now.*

I turned my head, so I couldn't see either of them.

"Well?" said Master Prosper.

Smile. "Clean as a whistle," I said. "Nothing in there except the future Duke of Essen."

$$\sim$$

Actually. Little white lie there.

Which might explain the violence of His reaction on seeing me; also various other incidents in our relationship. Because it's true, we don't intervene when the damage we'd do to the host outweighs the damage caused by the infestation. Defeating the object of the exercise. Whose side, it could reasonably be asked, are we on, anyhow?

But—well. I'm—I was going to say, only human. On reflection, you may disagree.

It was still His fault, for bearing grudges. I grant you, I was a bit excessive, after that first time He tried to fit me up and kill me. I may have overstepped the line just a bit, with regard to the purely voluntary code of conduct we have in these matters. But what He did after that was—

Did I mention I have a sister? And my sister had a baby.

~

Genius is a word you hear far too often these days, like *hero* or *tragedy*. Properly speaking, following the criteria officially approved by the Studium's standing committee on nomenclature, there have been only two geniuses so far in the whole of history: Saloninus (of course) and Prosper of Schanz.

Saloninus I know nothing about, except that a lot of scholars now believe he never existed. But Master Prosper, arrogant pinhead and grandson of a goatherd, is a genius, or the word simply has no meaning. To hell with whether or not the Great Horse would eventually get cast in bronze; the sketches alone, scrawled onto a painted-over masterpiece of early Mannerist fresco with a stick of charcoal, were among the most sublime expressions of the human spirit I've ever come across. Now, whether the credit for that goes to him or to Her ... or maybe to both of them. There's a school of scholarly opinion that maintains (on what grounds, I have no idea) that They are incapable of creating anything. They can't die; neither can they impart life, either literally or metaphorically. If that's true, then the divine creations of Master Prosper must be, for want of a better word, a collaboration, just as man and woman are both needed to collaborate on a child. The alternative is that all that remarkable stuff was dreamed up and put into practice by that clown, on his own, unassisted—which, having met the man and spent a lot of time with him, I solemnly declare to be unthinkable.

A collaboration, between us and Them—enough to turn your stomach just thinking about it. But maybe that's what it takes to come up with something so un-speakably, unthinkably—impossibly—wonderful as the sketches for the great bronze horse, or the violin con-certo, or that extraordinary contraption of birchwood laths, feathers, and string that—if he ever gets around to building it—will turn a human being into a bird.

And if so, would it be too high a price to pay?

Speaking of impossible—I was there when he solved most of the major insurmountable difficulties in the cast-ing process. We were sitting in the cloister garden, on either side of a section of broken column, which served us as a table for our drinks and nibbles. He liked talking to me, he said, forgetting he'd already told me that; or rather, thinking aloud at me. I made him feel safe, and his mind could come out of its shell and soar, instead of cowering.

The weight of the molten metal bursting the mold was nothing, he told me. Simply do the casting in a deep pit, and let the walls of the pit support the sides of the mold. The balance problem? Obvious, really. Fit massive steel rods inside the hind legs of the horse, reaching from hoof to fetlock in one direction and the same length in the other; cut a screw thread on the lower section; the projecting ends of the pins pass through the marble plinth and are secured with washers the size of well-covers and gigantic nuts; thus the statue is bolted solid to the plinth, the ankles are reinforced so they won't snap or bend, and the length of the plinth supplies the balance. As for the problem of moving around these colossal weights: He'd happened to cast an eye over the inventory of the royal arsenal and noticed that somewhere, in a deep, dark shed, the Duke had forty-six trebuchets, mothballed in his father's time, when cannon first came in. Now, what is a trebuchet but an enormous crane, fitted with a substantial counterweight, and perfectly serviceable mechanisms for raising and lowering both counterweight and beam without undue effort through the proper application of mechanical advantage? A few simple modifications, and that would be that.

What about the differential cooling? I asked him. He smiled. He'd given that a lot of thought, he said, and then it suddenly came to him, out of the blue, like (his own simile) being shat on by a seagull. Into the plaster core, insert a network of coiled copper pipes, through which cold water can be continually circulated during the actual pouring of the metal, thereby making sure that the outside and the inside of the bronze cools at approximately the same rate.

Genius, I said. He tried to look modest. Well. Nobody, not even Master Prosper, can be expected to succeed at everything.

Which just leaves, I said, the coating of the inside of the initial mold with wax. Which, unless you can think of a way of picking the mold up and swirling it around—

He scowled at me, and She smirked. *He's a clever boy,* She whispered. *He'll think of something.*

∿

Scruples. You may remember, I volunteered my lack of such as my contribution to the partnership.

It all depends on how badly you want something; in

this case, the success of the project. A few years ago, it was revenge, or (a bit less melodramatically) to get my own back on Him for trying to have me killed. As I said, I may have overreacted slightly. That was His excuse, the next time I met Him, inside the head of my sister's three-month-old daughter.

It's the only place where I know I'll be safe, He said.

You may also recall that when one of Them gets inside an infant, it's horribly dangerous to the host to evict it before the child reaches a certain age, usually two or three years before the onset of puberty. *I give you my word,* He said, *I'll bide here nice and quiet, nobody will know I'm here, I won't hurt her, I'll just curl up in a ball and go to sleep, like a squirrel.*

I was too angry to say anything. I'd warned Him, over and over again: Leave my family alone. Play your nasty games with me, if you have to; but if you do anything to them, anything at all, then so help me— And He'd taken no notice. Making a big show of being terrified, but really just laughing at me.

When you're being trained, they give you various no-win scenarios, to see how you react. One of them is a very strong demon firmly dug in to a very weak, vulnerable host. Getting It out would kill the host, no question about it. So what do you do? Leave It in there, to torture and agonize a fellow human being, for as long as the malevolent intruder can keep the physical body alive, purely and simply for the purpose of suffering torment? You have to use your own judgment, they tell you. No good can come of the situation. You have to choose the lesser evil. And if you listen to your scruples, the bleatings of conscience and its misguided appeals to the basic standards of our common humanity, you could well allow a greater evil because you shrink from getting your hands red with a lesser one.

I learned that lesson well. Ten out of ten, alpha double plus, and a commendation.

Afterwards, my sister said it wasn't my fault. I'd done all I could—somehow she'd got the impression that I was a medical doctor—and I wasn't to blame myself.

And I didn't. I don't. I blame Him.

⁓

The horse had to succeed. It would mean so much. It would mean everything.

We live in a miserable world, where the best we can honestly hope for is that one empty, meaningless day will follow another without things getting actively worse. A great man once said that the beating of the heart and the action of the lungs are a useful prevarication, keeping all options open. It's a good line (though it doesn't scan properly, in the original), but it presupposes that at least some of the options are good. I'm not convinced. Maybe it's because I've spent so much of my life around immortals (creatures, by definition, of pure evil); the way I see it, when you've got only seventy-odd years maximum, and half of those are going to be spent gradually sliding downhill into arthritis and senility, how the hell can you expect to achieve anything worthwhile?

Unless you happen to be a genius, like Master Prosper. The idea that there are men like that, capable of fiddling around with paper, pens, paints, bits of rock, and using that rubbish to create things so wonderful that even a soul-dead idiot like me has to stop and take his hat off and stare in wonder—it makes you doubt your etched-in-the-bone pessimism, just a little, just for a moment. Only Master Prosper never finishes anything; whereupon we can all say that that proves our point. He gets good ideas, but life is too short.

To put it another way, more concise and less whinging: only two things live forever, the instruments of darkness and works of genius. Which, I now had disturbingly good reason to believe, might not be such separate categories as I'd once thought. Collaborations.

(Good word. Two artists collaborate on a masterpiece. Traitors collaborate with the enemy.)

Therefore, the horse *had* to succeed, to show that the impossible could be done, and that occasionally, works of genius do get finished. But how—how, in God's name—do you apply a three-inch coating of wax to the inside of a mold for a colossal statue of a prancing horse?

~

Differential cooling, Master Prosper suggested. Molten wax cools faster against the edges than in the middle. So, fill the mold with liquid wax, and pump it out again.

We tried it, on a one-tenth scale model. Disaster. The wax cooled and went solid inside the hoses of the pump; and with hot wax, you only get so much time. Result: a quarter of the way down, the ample coating on the sides of the mold turned into a solid block. Solid block meant no core, no core meant no water-cooling, meant the whole thing would crumble into bits as soon as the clay was chipped off. Can't be done. Some things are possible; others aren't. Simple as that.

How about, Master Prosper suggested, cutting a hole in the top of the mold and reaching inside with a paintbrush on a very, very long handle? We tried that on the small model. It 40 percent worked, which is to say it 60 percent failed. There were too many bits where a straight long handle simply wouldn't reach, and hot wax runny enough to apply with a paintbrush won't stick properly to the sides. You'd have to get a man inside, I pointed out, and have him knead half-soft wax into the cracks and crevices with his thumb. And, of course, you couldn't get a man in there. Not enough room.

Stupid, isn't it? You solve half a dozen insuperable difficulties, so why can't you solve just one more? Because some things are possible, and some aren't. Simple as that.

~

But the horse had to succeed. So I made an excuse, and went hunting.

As luck would have it, the first one I ran into was an old sparring partner; we must have run into each other a dozen times over the years. It knew me very well.

Fine, It said as It saw me scowling in at It through some poor devil's eyes. *I give up. I'll go quietly.*

No, you won't, I said. *I've got a job for you.*

You what?

You're going to do something for me, I said. *Or I'll hurt you so badly you'll remember the pain every day for the rest of your everlasting life.*

Two pale eyes gazed at me. If I'd been capable of pity, I'd have felt it. *You're serious, aren't you?*

About the job, yes. And the pain.

Completely stunned. Tens of thousands of years of existence, you think you've heard it all, but apparently not. *You want me to help you?*

I nodded. *Collaboration,* I told It. *It's the next big thing.*

~

I'd already suggested it, minus one salient detail, to Master Prosper, but he hadn't been interested. Yes, he said, a five-year-old child (a particularly small, skinny one) might just fit inside; but first, where would you find a kid who'd go in there without fainting or dying of fright; and even if you found one, you couldn't possibly trust a kid to do the sort of careful, thorough, skillful job we'd need him to do. Forget it, he said. It's a nice thought, but impractical.

So I went away, and then I came back, leading by the hand a five-year-old girl. She was mine; I'd paid good money for her, in a back alley in Poor Town where you can buy *anything.*

Master Prosper was horrified. "You did what?"

"For the project," I said. "For the horse."

He struggled with himself; and while he was doing it,

She was demanding to know what I thought I was playing at. But I wasn't talking to Her.

"It'll be fine," I said. "Think about it. If I hadn't bought her, she'd have led a nasty, brutish, short life in Poor Town and probably be dead at thirty. Instead, she does a quick, simple job for us—not pleasant, but not exactly torture either—and the Duke settles money on her, she grows up well fed and educated and marries an army officer. We're actually doing her a favor."

He gave me an agonized look. "What makes you think," he said, "she'll go in there? Or do a proper job?"

"Leave that to me."

"But that's—"

"Don't ask."

"What do you mean, don't—?"

"Don't ask."

He went white as a sheet.

~

Master Prosper's authorized biographers (two of them; one or the other on duty round the clock, day and night) had been part of the royal marriage settlement, to be paid for, naturally, by the Duke. Accordingly they were, strictly speaking, public employees, and therefore had to be accredited members of the Notaries' Guild, whose members take a solemn oath to tell the truth.

But not necessarily the whole truth. For one thing, there simply isn't room, in a book that anyone could ever be expected to lift, let alone read; not for every last detail. Some things, no matter how true, get left out, inevitably. So the account of the casting of the Great Horse lists some of the insuperable problems that the great man overcame and the measures taken to overcome them, but not all. Space does not permit, and so forth.

I see what you meant about scruples, She said to me. We were back on speaking terms, just about.

You were the one who convinced me of the merits of this collaboration idea, I told Her.

Absolutely, She said. *Even so.*

As well as notaries, the biographers are also fully paid-up associates of the College of Authors, so their description of the casting of the Great Horse is much, much better than anything I could come up with. Look it up, enjoy, be suitably inspired. It's an amazing story, of obstacles overcome, dreams made real, abstract perfection trapped in a blob of metal like a fly in amber, and if they hadn't done it justice, they'd have deserved to have their legs broken. After all, the making of that story was expensive, even though the end result absolutely justified the means.

I can't describe what it looked like, when the cranes winched it out of the pit—still unfettled and unpolished, gritty and dull from the mold, with the sprues still branching out of it, as though it had been stored all winter and started to sprout. Even so, it was, quite literally, staggering. I turned to Master Prosper and said, "The best thing ever," and I meant it too.

He—they—looked at me. Couldn't say anything, because it wasn't something any of us would talk about, ever, to anyone. But words weren't necessary. We all understood.

~

Anyway, it rose up out of the pit, and was mounted on rollers and hauled into the enormous shed they'd built to house it while it was cleaned up and polished, ahead of the grand unveiling ceremony, in the presence of the royal family, the great man himself, and the entire ruling nobility of the nation. The day before the ceremony, my old friend the chaplain came back from his far-distant posting to bless the statue. I met him outside the shed; it was just starting to get dark. There were four or five heavily laden carts outside, and a small bunch of carters.

~

I didn't attend the actual unveiling ceremony, which was just as well.

The account in the official biography makes thrilling reading, especially the bit when, at high noon precisely, the Great Horse exploded like a cannon shell, blowing out a crater a quarter of an acre across and raining fragments of bronze shrapnel over half the city. The entire royal family was killed instantly, along with Prosper of Schanz and the flower of all Essen.

To this day, nobody knows who was responsible for filling the inside of the horse with gunpowder, though naturally the finger of suspicion points at the leaders of the Republican faction, who immediately took control of the Duchy and continue in power to this day. Nor—not that it matters, unless you have a morbid taste for technical trivia—has anyone ever been able to explain how the bomb was set off, since a burning fuse would have been painfully obvious, with all the security attending such an event.

Actually, I can explain that. After we sawed a hole in the top of the horse's head and poured in the powder, thirty-five barrels of the stuff, I replaced the horse's enamel eyes with glass ones, which I'd had specially made, following a design in Prosper's *Principles of Mathe-*

matics; the section on burning glasses. I knew where the horse would be at precisely noon, and also the sun. The rest was simple optics. Soldering the top of the head back on was a ticklish business, with all that powder in there, but we got away with it.

The Great Horse was very beautiful indeed. The mythical version of it, which will survive in people's imaginations until there are no more humans left on earth, will be many, many times lovelier, and its effect infinitely more powerful and inspiring. Moral: you can blow up a statue, and its creator, but you can't kill goodness and beauty. Which is another way of saying that the greatest force for good in this world is, of course, Art, especially Art filled with high explosives. I think Master Prosper would have liked that.

(You see, I could have dragged Him out of the Prince, which would have killed the Prince, but then the Duke would've had me hanged, and She'd have got away free. Or I could have thrown Her out of Master Prosper, and She'd have killed Prosper on the way out—the gallows for me, and the Prince would've grown up with my old friend lodged inside him. One but not both—if it hadn't been for Prosper's wonderful horse.)

I met Him again, not long after. He told me He'd lodged an official complaint about me with the proper authorities. Bloody cheek, which I've since given Him

100

reason to regret.

And the grand design goes on, presumably, in some form or other, world without end, amen. But not on my watch.

About the Author

Having worked in journalism, numismatics, and the law, K. J. Parker now writes for a precarious living.

K. J. Parker also writes under the name Tom Holt.

TOR·COM

**Science fiction. Fantasy. The universe.
And related subjects.**

*

More than just a publisher's website, *Tor.com*
is a venue for **original fiction, comics,** and
discussion of the entire field of SF and fantasy,
in all media and from all sources. Visit our site
today — and join the conversation yourself.

CPSIA information can be obtained
at www.ICGtesting.com
Printed in the USA
LVHW090318170420
653809LV00006B/1864